W9-BGB-214

When This Box Is Full

By
Patricia Lillie

Pictures by
Donald Crews

Greenwillow Books
New York

Text copyright © 1993
by Patricia Lillie.
Illustrations copyright
© 1993 by Donald Crews.

Printed in Hong Kong by
South China Printing
Company (1988) Ltd.
First Edition
10 9 8 7 6 5 4 3 2 1

The black-and-white
photographs were reproduced
from line conversions screened
with a "Lasergrain" pattern.
Color was added by hand with
film overlays. The text type is
Helvetica Black Italic.

Library of Congress
Cataloging-in-Publication Data
Lillie, Patricia.
When this box is full /
by Patricia Lillie;
pictures by Donald Crews.
        p.   cm.
Summary: Each month a child
adds something to an empty
box, including a red foil heart in
February and toasted pumpkin
seeds in October.
ISBN 0-688-12016-4 (trade).
ISBN 0-688-12017-2 (lib. bdg.)
[1. Months—fiction.]
I. Crews, Donald, ill.
II. Title.
PZ7.L632Wi   1993
[E]—dc20
92-28743   CIP   AC

Endpaper boxes
from Donald Crews's
private collection

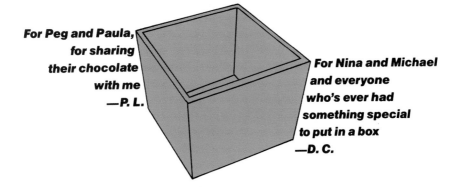

For Peg and Paula,
for sharing
their chocolate
with me
—P. L.

For Nina and Michael
and everyone
who's ever had
something special
to put in a box
—D. C.

**This box
is empty...
but not
for long.**

**I will fill
it with...**

January

a snowman's scarf,

January
February
March

**a red
foil heart,**

a robin's
feather,

January
February
March
April

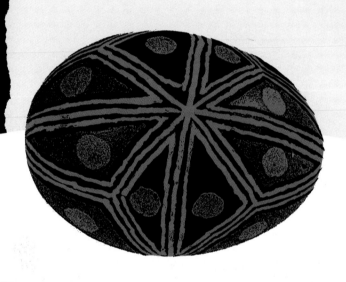

**a purple
eggshell,**

January
February
March
April
May
June

a wild
daisy,

helicopters from the maple tree,

January

February

March

April

May

June

July

a seashell
and some
sand,

January
February
March
April
May
June
July
August

a ribbon
from
the fair,

January
February
March
April
May
June
July
August
September

a red leaf,

January

February

March

April

May

June

July

August

September

October

**toasted
pumpkin
seeds,**

January
February
March
April
May
June
July
August
September
October
November
December

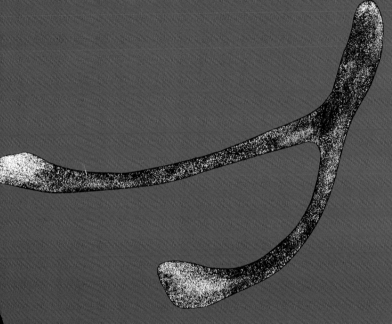

a wishbone,

and
a silver
star.

And then...

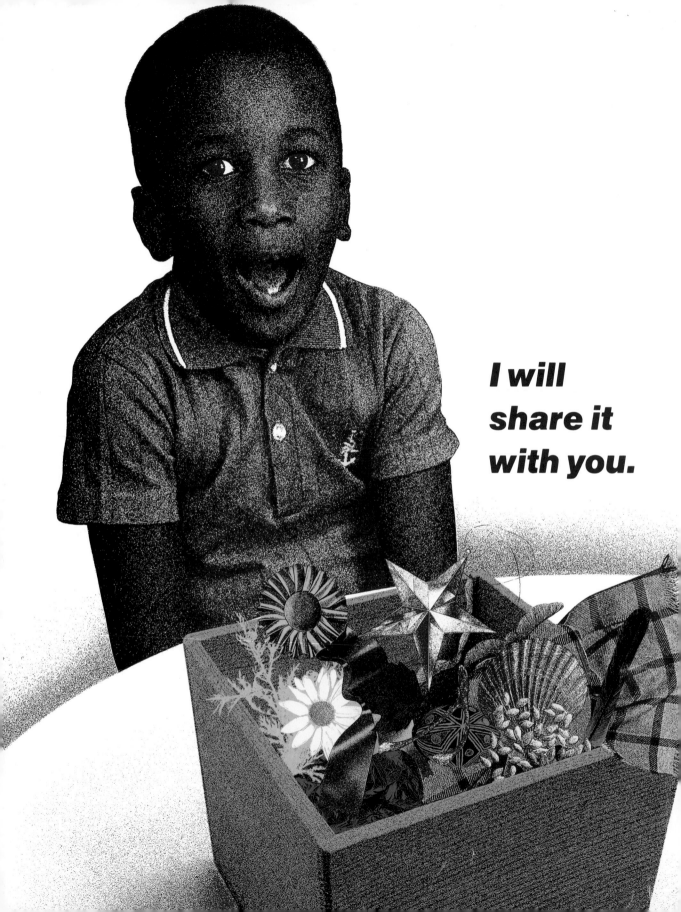